JP
HES

Hest, Amy.

Weekend girl.

$14.93

DATE			

9/93

BAKER & TAYLOR BOOKS

Weekend Girl

Amy Hest

Illustrated by Harvey Stevenson

Morrow Junior Books   New York

Windsor and Newton watercolors and pencil were used for the full-color artwork.
The text type is 15-point Garamond.

Inquiries should be addressed to
William Morrow and Company, Inc.,
1350 Avenue of the Americas, New York, NY 10019.
Printed in Hong Kong by South China Printing Company (1988) Ltd.

1   2   3   4   5   6   7   8   9   10

Library of Congress Cataloging-in-Publication Data
Hest, Amy.
Weekend girl / Amy Hest; illustrations by Harvey Stevenson.   p.   cm.
Summary: When her parents go away for the weekend, Sophie enjoys
sharing her grandfather's hobby and her grandmother's picnic while
she stays with them in New York City.
ISBN 0-688-09689-1 (TR).—ISBN 0-688-09690-5 (LE)
[1. Grandparents—Fiction.   2. New York (N.Y.)—Fiction.
3. Photography—Fiction.]   I. Stevenson, Harvey, ill.   II. Title.
PZ7.H4375We   1993
[E]—dc20   92-9193   CIP   AC

For Alyson and Cory, with love
— A. H.

For Walker and Jenny
— H. S.

Toward the end of summer, when the grass needs cutting and wildflowers stretch from here to the barn and back again, my parents take their private, no-kid vacation.

Off they go, just the two of them, for three days and a couple of nights. They drive north to the mountains, or south, or west. This year, they are going somewhere really special, to a cottage by the sea. Ten years ago, my parents honeymooned there…and long before that, my grandparents did, too!

They pack the old brown suitcase until it bulges.

They pack up all the dogs to visit neighbors—except for one, my Shaker.

Then they pack up me, to visit Gram and Grampa in New York City.

This car is stuffed and overstuffed and we are bumping down the graveled driveway. Shaker's ears, and his whiskers, blow back in the breeze. He howls away. I twist around for a last look at the house and my bedroom window. "See you later," I whisper through my fingers. Then I blow a kiss.

We drive and drive. My parents chatter in the front seat. I
write a poem in the backseat and ask, "Are we there yet? Are
we in the city?" And they say, "Soon, Sophie."

They talk about Honeymoon Cottage, windswept and
crooked, just steps from the sea.

They remember a storm and the wild, rolling ocean that slapped against their woody porch. I take a fuzzy peach from the bag and we drive.

A long time later, we cross the bridge to the city. A thousand goose bumps dance up my arms, then dance down again.

Gram and Grampa live in a redbrick apartment house high
on a hill near the Hudson River. The elevator creaks. Shaker
and I head straight for the stairs and race each other all the
way to six. Grampa is always waiting in the hallway. He loves
to tickle my cheek with his mustache. And he loves to tease my
parents, like this:

"I see you are leaving this bad kid behind. What do you
think, we like her or something?"

"She's all yours, Dad." My mother teases back, waggling a
finger under his nose. "But just until Sunday. We need our
Sophie back with us on Sunday."

Gram's ballet slippers make a shuffling sound on the old wood floors. "Hello, weekend girl!" She squeezes me hard and kisses both my cheeks. Her dress is long to her ankles, and cherry-colored, and swingy. She always wears them swingy, and she always has a checklist for my parents. "The car is packed? You have ponchos and an extra sweater? You have a thermos and a map, and you will drive slowly on those hairpin turns…?"

"Grampa?" I tug his sleeve. "Is there a surprise, like always," I whisper, "one that you and Gram dream up just for me?"

"Hmm…I don't know." Grampa twirls the pointy tips of

his mustache. "How on earth do we top last year's circus, Sophie, or the Statue of Liberty the year you were four...?"

I don't know how to top those. All the same, I hope they're planning something. There is nothing quite like a city surprise.

I slip my father an envelope marked FOR SOPHIE'S PARENTS, DO NOT OPEN UNTIL YOU GET TO HONEYMOON COTTAGE. Inside is my best poem ever. It's about a baby bear and I call it "Homesick, Sometimes."

A round of good-byes, and they are gone.

Shaker licks my fingers. He always licks my fingers when he's sad.

Then Grampa says, "I need a helper in the darkroom. Under nine is best. She might even have a freckle!" He steers me down the hallway to the back end of the apartment, where he has a special room for making pictures.

My grandfather has a camera with a million gadgets, and he takes the best pictures of anyone I know. They are all over the apartment, and all over my country house, too. His favorite subject is Gram. Everywhere you look, there are pictures of Gram teaching her ballet class.

I love everything about the darkroom, including Grampa's green plaid workshirt and the smell of the chemical solutions and the little red light bulb that hangs from the ceiling. There's a funny old radio that might be a family heirloom. Grampa lets me work right alongside him, and he never says things like "Don't touch, Sophie" or "This is strictly for grown-ups."

I swoosh and pat, swoosh and pat. Suddenly, Gram is in the picture. "It's magic." I wave my silvery tongs. "Everything here is like magic!"

Later we eat knuckle cookies at the big kitchen table. My grandmother's knuckles are better than any cookies anywhere. The recipe is a family secret.

"I know you two are planning a surprise." I munch away. "You always do; it's like a tradition."

Gram dips a cookie in her coffee. Grampa stirs sugar into his.

"How about a hint?" I say. "A person whose parents go off

for a weekend without her, a person like that *deserves* a hint."

"Tomorrow," they say.

"That's too long." I pour milk from the pitcher and I pout. "My parents must miss me," I say.

"I bet they are talking about you this very minute." Gram tucks a strand of hair behind my ear. "I bet they are saying something wonderful."

In the morning, Gram and I take Shaker to Riverside Park.
He runs wild and free.

"The city is fun, Gram, and different, but I miss my house
and my room."

"I know what you mean. When I visit you in the country"
—Gram nods—"I miss my house and my room, too."

"Tell me about your Honeymoon Cottage. Please," I say.

"I remember every detail." Gram smiles. "Even back then, it was old and crooked. But cozy, like a dollhouse, Sophie. It smelled just slightly of lilacs, which I kept in a vase on the kitchen table. There was a stone fireplace, a screened porch..." Gram's voice drifts off. "And storms galore! Splendid summer storms the year we were married."

"Did Grampa take pictures?"

"The best pictures ever." Gram takes a bow like a real ballerina.

"My mother says you were some good dancer when you were young."

"When I was young was a long time ago." Gram whistles for Shaker while I run ahead, flapping my arms at a spotted pigeon.

All through the day, Gram prepares for the surprise. She roasts. She bakes. And I say, "What time do we leave?" She packs up macaroni salad, and chicken, and potato salad, and I say, "Do we take a subway to get there?" She cuts lemon pound cake into wedges. "Uptown or downtown?" I say as she fills the wicker basket.

When we leave, it is late afternoon. Gram and Grampa carry
the basket between them, and we walk. We walk and walk—
past six Broadway grocers, eleven newsstands, two ice-cream
shops, one very fancy sneaker shop, one plain-regular sneaker
shop, five Chinese restaurants, one movie theater, one deli

with a line of people out the door, and one hot-bagel shop that smells fantastic. We walk and they talk about the fun of surprises, and I say, "Are we there yet?" And they answer, "Soon, Sophie. We'll be there soon." I wish we'd stopped for a bagel.

The sign says CENTRAL PARK. NO CARS TONIGHT. We follow curvy roads that wind and twist, then straighten for awhile. There are up hills and down hills, but mostly they go up. And people—I've never seen so many people all in one place! They are tall and short and wide and narrow. They are old and young and in-between. And everyone is just like us, lugging and pulling, tugging and dragging blankets and baskets and shopping bags that look like art.

"First star!" calls Gram. "Make a wish, Sophie!"

"I wish I could sit and rest these poor tired legs."

We veer off the road, through a little wood. Beyond is a great green lawn and it is packed—every single inch of it, I guess—with people. Finally we stop.

Our blanket is navy blue. It used to be my mother's camp blanket. We flap it up and smooth it down and plant our shoes at all four corners. Then we feast...and feast...and feast! The sun slips behind a jagged row of buildings. I eat so much my

stomach pops out. I lie back and watch the sky turn colors.
There's a lot of pink and yellow. It looks nearly like a
country sky.

"This place is grand," I say, "and the food is delicious!"
Grampa takes my picture. Then he takes two more.

Gram fidgets, then she fishes in the picnic basket. She pulls out a photograph, smallish, oldish, and scalloped at the edges. The girl in the picture is laughing. "Her bathing suit reminds me of an old-time movie," I say. "I *love* her straw hat, and look how the ocean curls at her toes! I like her."

I keep inspecting the photograph. "She certainly is pretty," I decide.

"It's no wonder." Grampa beams. "That lovely lady is your *grandmother!* And there in the back, that's Honeymoon Cottage!"

"I wasn't bad looking, if I must say." Gram shrugs but her cheeks are pink and her eyes are dancing.

"Can I have it?" I whisper. "Can I have it for keeps?"

"We thought you'd never ask."

Well, Grampa takes pictures of everything. All around, everywhere, is a feeling that something special is about to happen. Soon it does.

Far away, across the big green lawn, musicians step up to a high stage. The music comes softly at first. It rises, sinks, and

floats around the rows of trees. It rises, sinks, and floats among
the hush of people. I lean against Shaker and I listen.

I think about my parents at Honeymoon Cottage. Maybe I
will go there, too, one day, and there better be a storm so I can
watch the wild ocean spray that woody porch. . . .

All around us, city lights flicker. But here in this spot, it is
nearly pitch-black. I tingle all over at the night and the stars,
and Gram and Grampa holding hands.

Shaker sniffs my foot and the music plays on.